The Grey Men

DAVID ORME

Rans♦m

The Grey Men
by David Orme
Illustrated by Jorge Mongiovi and Ulises Carpintero
Cover photographs: © Clint Spencer and Lee Pettet

Published by Ransom Publishing Ltd.
Radley House, 8 St. Cross Road, Winchester, Hampshire SO23 9HX
www.ransom.co.uk

ISBN   978 184167 455 1

First published in 2011

Originally published in 1998 by Stanley Thornes Publishers Ltd.

A CIP catalogue record of this book is available from the British Library.

Printed and bound in India by Nutech Print Services

CONTENTS

NOT FOR THE PUBLIC TO KNOW
TOP SECRET
ZONE 13 FILES ONLY

A CLOSE ENCOUNTER

Martin and Jade were out late. They had been to see a friend in the next village. Now they were cycling home.

It was a very dark night. There was no moon. They went as fast as they could.

'Mum and Dad are going to be really mad,' said Jade. 'We will be grounded for a week.'

Martin knew his sister was right. They had never been this late before.

Just then it seemed to get lighter. Jade stopped and looked up at the sky.

'What's that?' she said. 'I've never seen a plane like that.'

There was a strange object in the sky. It was round, and covered with lights. The lights were flashing on and off. Sometimes they were red, sometimes they were yellow. It stopped still in the sky over the road in front of them.

'It's a UFO!' yelled Martin. 'You know, a flying saucer!'

Jade didn't believe in flying saucers. At least, she hadn't until now.

NOT FOR THE PUBLIC TO KNOW
TOP SECRET
ZONE 13 FILES ONLY

INTO THE SPACESHIP

The UFO started to move. It came slowly towards them. Soon it was right over their heads. A beam of white light shot down. It was so bright they were almost blinded.

Jade and Martin felt very strange. They couldn't move their arms or legs!

Suddenly they felt themselves being pulled up. They heard their bikes falling over with a crash. They were heading upwards towards the UFO!

They were soon past the tree tops. Higher and higher they went. Jade guessed that they were being captured. She was terrified.

She tried to look up at the UFO but she couldn't move her head.

There must have been a door in the bottom of the UFO. It was very bright inside. They heard a clang as the door shut under them.

They still couldn't move.

There were strange people waiting. They were small, with a smooth, grey skin. They had big, black eyes.

Jade and Martin were grabbed by strong hands. They tried to cry out but they couldn't make a sound. Soon they were strapped down. They could only look upwards. Jade could see a big machine above her. The machine had a large, sharp needle.

The needle was coming down, down – straight at her face!

NOT FOR THE PUBLIC TO KNOW
TOP SECRET
ZONE 13 FILES ONLY

3

WHERE HAVE YOU BEEN?

The needle stopped just a centimetre from her face. Jade heard a hiss. A gas came out of the needle. Jade felt very cold. The cold crept all over her body. She felt dizzy. There was a roaring sound in her ears. Slowly she fell asleep. Would she ever wake up? This was her last thought.

000//000

Martin woke up first. He was lying on the grass by the side of the road. His sister was lying next to him.

Martin gave his sister a shove.

'Jade, wake up!'

Jade slowly woke up.

'I had a terrible dream,' she said.

'If that was a dream, I had it too,' said Martin.

'What time is it? My watch has stopped,' said Jade.

'Mine has stopped too!'

Jade picked up her bike.

'We had better hurry,' she said. 'Don't say anything about it to Mum and Dad. They would only say we were lying.'

Just then they saw a car's headlights. That was Dad's car!

Dad was very angry.

'Where have you been?' he shouted. 'It's three o'clock in the morning! Your mum is frantic!'

They piled the bikes in the back of the car and got in. Three in the morning! They had left their friend's house at ten o'clock. What had happened to them in the UFO?

THE NEXT NIGHT

Martin and Jade were grounded for a long time. Jade didn't mind too much. She was scared to go out in case she met the UFO again.

The next night Jade had a strange dream. It was one of those dreams that seemed almost real.

She was back in the UFO. The grey men were standing round her, looking down at her. They didn't speak, but Jade knew what they

wanted to say. She could hear their thoughts in her brain.

'We are looking for the right people,' the grey men were thinking. 'We need people to come with us. Space is a wonderful place. It is full of excitement and danger! Leave your world. Come with us!'

Jade woke suddenly. She was screaming, 'No! No!'

Her parents rushed in to see what the matter was. She told them she had had a nightmare. She wouldn't tell them what it was about.

ooo//ooo

Next morning, Martin spoke to her.

'I heard you shouting in the night. You had the dream, too, didn't you?'

Jade nodded.

'It was horrible! I couldn't bear to leave home and go away with those horrible creatures.'

Martin didn't say anything.

BACK TO THE UFO

Jade couldn't get to sleep that night. She was terrified in case the dream came again. She was even more worried about the grey men from the UFO. What if they came to get her while she was asleep?

She made sure her window was locked. She guessed that the grey men could still get in if they wanted to.

She tried to read her book. She kept
thinking about the UFO. She got up and
looked out of the window.

In the distance, over the trees, she could see
lights. They were flashing. She knew those
lights. The UFO was back!

It was getting closer and closer. Jade
wanted to hide her head under the bedclothes.
She was sure it was coming for her!

Then she heard something outside. She
opened the window and looked out. Martin
had got out of his bedroom window and was
climbing down the drainpipe!

'What are you doing?' Jade whispered as
loudly as she could. 'Come back!'

Martin took no notice. He reached the
ground. A minute later he set off on his bike
towards the UFO.

Jade got dressed quickly. She had to stop
Martin! She ran downstairs and opened the

back door. Soon she was cycling along the road. She could see Martin ahead of her.

The UFO was getting nearer. Suddenly, the great beam of light shone down. She heard a crash as Martin's bike fell over. She saw him being pulled up towards the UFO!

6

THE BRIGHT LIGHT

Jade rushed towards the light. It was really blinding. She couldn't see anything at all.

She didn't know how long she stood in the bright light. She was weeping. Why had Martin done it? Whatever could she tell her parents?

Then she saw a dark figure. It was walking towards her. She was terrified. It must be one of the grey men. They had taken Martin – now they were coming for her!

She wanted to run away, but she was so terrified her legs refused to move. At last she managed to cry out.

'Please! Leave me alone! I just want to go home!'

The dark figure came closer, and Jade almost fell down with relief. It wasn't one of the grey men. It was too tall for that. It was her brother!

Martin walked towards her. He seemed to be in a state of shock.

'I wanted to go,' he said. 'But they wouldn't take me!'

'But why?' screamed Jade. She wanted to shake her brother. 'How could you think of going off with those horrible creatures?'

'I wanted to see space,' said Martin. 'I wanted to see all the wonderful things in the dream. But I wasn't the person they wanted. I wasn't right for them.'

'What do you mean?' said Jade.

'It's not me they want. It's you.'

Jade started to scream again. She felt herself being pulled upwards into the UFO.

Then she couldn't scream any more.

NOT FOR THE PUBLIC TO KNOW

TOP SECRET

ZONE 13 FILES ONLY

ABOUT THE AUTHOR

David Orme is an expert on strange, unexplained events. For his protection (and yours) we cannot show a photograph of him.

David created the Zone 13 files to record the cases he studied. Some of these files really do involve aliens, but many do not. Aliens are not everywhere. Just in most places.

These stories are all taken from the Zone 13 files. They will not be here for long. Read them while you can.

But don't close your eyes when you go to sleep at night. **They** will be watching you.